Sandcastles

Lily Lawson

THE
WRIGHT HOUSE

Published by
The Wright House.

Cover design
by Dreena Collins

By The Author

Poetry Books

My Fathers Daughter,
A Taste of What's to Come,
Rainbow's Red Book of Poetry
Rainbow's Orange Book of Poetry

Kids' Books

Santa's Early Christmas,
The Palm Tree Swingers Island Band
If I Were Invisible…

Short Stories

Sandcastles

Contents

Unexpected

Love, Andy

I woke cold and wet, buried in a snow drift. I shook myself, attempting to defrost and escape my prison before the ice took hold and mummified me.

I was on the streets because I was no longer considered cute. My adopted family's affection for me evaporated with the discovery that having brought home a puppy, they soon owned a dog.

After digging for a while it became easier, someone was helping me. A glove-wearing human was digging from the other side.

When my freedom was restored, the human reached out her hand and I sniffed it. She brushed my fur, removing the chunks of snow my shaking refused to shift. I was grateful for the warmth of her touch.

I don't know how I ended up where I was. I had been wandering the streets taking shelter where I could find it for longer than I cared to think about.

'My goodness it's cold. You can't stay out here on the streets, you'll die. Where's home?'

My rescuer's voice was kind. Home? I wouldn't call the last place I lived home. Not any more anyway.

'You can't tell me? Well, you better come home with me then. Some food and water and a roof over your head will be better than wandering about out here in this.'

She beckoned for me to follow her.

Home, food, water? I wanted all of those … I hesitated. I had trusted before, and it didn't end well. Who was to say it wouldn't happen again?

The chill in my bones and empty stomach fought with my wish not to rely on another human ever again.

'I'm Olivia. What's your name?'

My name? I couldn't tell her. It was a long time since anyone had called me anything at all; well, nothing worth repeating in polite company. The dogs I met wore collars with name tags. My owners hadn't stretched to that. The language barrier and the fact I'd lost my voice didn't help matters.

Olivia's eyes met mine.

'Nothing to tell me? Well, my friend, I have to call you something. Let me see.'

Friend? That sounded good.

She paused to take me in, her furrowed brow and lip-biting told me she was thinking.

'How about Andy? It is St Andrews Day, after all.'

I nodded. Wow, I wish I had my voice. I liked her choice. It sounded friendly, and at least I had a name.

***

Olivia's home was warm. She gave me food and water before leaving me to lie in front of the fire. I must have fallen asleep. The next thing I knew it was dark.

I got to my feet and padded to the door, not wishing to outstay my welcome.

'Andy, do you want to go out?' Olivia came and opened the door. I lifted my paw, and she took it.

Out? Yes, please. I don't want to be punished for making a mess on the floor.

Another goodbye. This one better than the last. At least I was fed and watered. Being warm and able to get some rest helped too. I was leaving with dignity on my own legs, not shoved out with harsh words ringing in my ears.

'Don't be too long. It's cold out there and the sky is full of snow. Wouldn't want you to get buried again, would we?'

Hang on a minute. What's happening here?

Olivia stood in the doorway, arms crossed while I did what I had to do.

Unsure, I looked at her sideways waiting for her next move. Was she teasing me? I swished my tail. She opened the door wide.

'Come on Andy, it's freezing.' She beckoned me over.

Come, Andy? Why? It is cold. She had that right. What was she going to do to me?

I crept toward the open door, expecting her to shut it in my face. She was letting me back inside?

I inched my way into the kitchen, alert and ready to run back out again. Had she gone to get something to hit me? I don't think I did anything wrong. Humans are hard to read. I think I am being good, then they get angry. Her hands were empty, and she was smiling at me, a happy smile.

'One step at a time Andy,' the voice in my head cautioned.

She came over to me. Her voice had not lost its kindness. I am not sure I can trust Olivia although I haven't made her mad yet.

'That's right, come back in the warm. I've borrowed food and treats for you from my neighbour. I hope you like them. I'll get some more in a couple of days when the weather gets a bit better.'

Olivia held a box I didn't recognise and pulled something out of it.

Warm? Yes, it was much nicer in the warm house. Treats? I had heard of those; my friends with the collars got them. I was lucky if my owners fed me.

She held out her hand, and I took the offering. It did taste good, and I was still hungry. I licked her hand to thank her, and she gave me another one. I was being thoroughly spoilt today.

'Don't get used to it,' the voice inside my head warned me.

'Andy, this is your cupboard.' Olivia opened a door in her kitchen. 'We'll have to find out what food you like. It's been a long time since I've had a canine friend. I think I can remember what's good. This is your home now; I want you to be happy.'

Food? Friend? Home? Happy? I loved the sound of that.

She bent down and hugged me.

Home? I ran the word through my head to see if it fitted. It did feel safe here. Much better than the streets and I had nowhere else to go. It was worth sticking around a bit longer to give it a chance.

***

That was nine months ago.

I kept doubting. She won me round. She keeps saying she loves me; it's like she knows I need to keep hearing it. I have a collar with my name on it and her phone number. 'In case I get lost,' she said.

I have my voice back now. I do my best to tell her I love her too.
We don't speak the same language, but I think she knows.

Dog Gone Cute

I was putting one last dog biscuit on the treat kennel I'd built for national dog day when an excitable golden Labrador bounded into the store. Much as I love dogs, I didn't adore this one wreaking havoc on my display. Well, on the bits he wasn't eating.

'Where's your owner?'

'That'll be me.' A tall, tousled blond stood in the doorway; a dog lead draped around his neck.

I opened my mouth to shout. His blue eyes stole my anger and replaced it with, 'Don't worry, it's OK.'

I was gone. And so was he before I knew his name.

The Dating Game

Without meaning to, she'd arranged two dates for the same evening on the opposite sides of town.

Mike thought she was into classical music and sushi. Sam thought she was into football and burgers. The truth was, she was into Mike and Sam. Her inability to choose between them and unwilling to be honest about it had led to this.

Debbie picked up her phone, tried to form words to send to one of them, failed, and continued cleaning the flat.

With knots in her stomach, she went through her wardrobe selecting appropriate clothing for both occasions.

Mike was lean and broody with eyes that made her melt. They talked about anything and everything. His broodiness led to arguments. He'd stomped off so often it was becoming a routine.

Sam was a gym bunny, affectionate and caring. He made her laugh. They had grown so comfortable together it unnerved her. She was sure she'd been friend zoned.

Did she want to get dressed in an evening gown and heels and eat sushi when she was starving?

Did she want to stand in the snow watching football for two hours?

She'd decided. She wasn't going anywhere.

The mobile phone signal wasn't working in the apartment building again, so Debbie donned her warmest coat and stood on the front steps.

She'd sent her texts and was about to go in when the gate squeaked.

James, her upstairs neighbour, was arriving home. His smile lit up his face.

'What are you doing out here? It's freezing.'

'Cancelling my plans. I can't be bothered to go anywhere.' Debbie hugged herself.

'It's a night for takeaway and Netflix for sure.' He rubbed his arms.

'Yup. I'm going to go get warm again.'

James held the door open.

'I've got Chinese. I always buy too much, there's more than enough if you want to join? It's an enormous sofa so loads of room.'

The smell emanating from the cartons had Debbie's stomach begging for attention.

'That sounds great.' She grinned. 'Lead the way.'

As James made his way upstairs ahead of her, Debbie couldn't help noticing how good his bum looked in his jeans.

***

Sat on the enormous sofa, a sliver of space between them, the sauce dripping from Debbie's mouth covered her drool at James' toned torso barely concealed by his shirt.

They discovered they had similar taste in films as the evening slipped by with the aid of red wine.

When they said goodnight, James brushed her cheek with his lips, as their hands touched.

'You owe me a takeaway,' he called as she left the flat.

Her laugh flew up the stairs.

He grinned.

Arriving at her door, she found a bunch of roses and a bucket of doughnuts each with a note.

Mike said he hoped she would get well soon.

Sam said he was sorry he'd missed her, hoped she was ok, and would ring later to check. He reminded her to please call if she needed anything.

She carried everything inside, wondering if James liked pizza.

Falling

She is falling and I can't stop her. She swims toward the ground, legs and arms trying to gain some direction. Gasps come from below. People are covering their eyes.

The intensifying heat means I can't hold off much longer. I have to know if she survives. If I take my focus off her, I might miss her last moment of beauty.

Sirens herald the arrival of fire engines.

The crowd have large blankets. They watch her body, moving as if in a video game. The prize is her life. Two firefighters join them. The rest prepare for the slow climb to the windows of the trapped.

I say a quick prayer and throw my tied sheets out the window, I should be able to get to the roof a few floors below. I don my gloves. I can't wait for rescue.

A cheer goes up from the ground. My girlfriend has been caught in the blanket. Relief floods through me.

I climb onto the ledge and take my first steps back to her waiting arms.

Unconditional

Cut the Mustard

Tommy mustered his courage, took a deep breath, and opened the door of the shop.

'What do you want, young man?' Mrs Blythe stood at the counter, arms folded as Tommy approached. Behind her, the assortment of regimented tins and packets appeared to join her in a scrutiny of their own.

Tommy's insides wanted to bolt for the door. His feet refused to budge.

'I were wondering like …' He fiddled with his tie. 'If there were any work going?'

The look she gave him could have curdled milk.

'Well, I have heard you got young Melissa in the family way, hmmm.' Mrs Blythe's eyes travelled the length of his body. 'I suppose at least you're not shirking your responsibilities. When's the wedding?'

'I dunno if …' Tommy's face grew red, his palms sweaty.

Mrs Blythe rolled her eyes. 'Nonsense; I'll have a word with the vicar. If she's not showing we might get away with it. Not sure about white mind. Maybe off-white or cream.' She tidied the counter.

'We might not be getting wed …'

She sighed.

'You scared of her dad? Billy Barker's a pussy cat.'

Tommy shuffled his feet.

'No, he's been alright wiv me considering, … Just, we dunno if we want all that?'

She hit the counter.

Tommy jumped.

Mrs Blythe leaned forward; her big bosom pressed to the shiny wood.

'No employee of mine is living over the brush. This is a respectable establishment, you think on.'

Tommy ran his eyes over the shelves behind her.

'You'll give us a job then?'

'Put a ring on Melissa's finger and I'll see what I can do.'

Tommy sighed.

'She mightn't want that; she mightn't want me.'

'Well, she should have thought of that before she let you have your fun. You didn't force yourself on her, did you?'

'I would never … Honest.' Tommy's face lit up like a stop sign.

'No, you don't seem the type. Just had to be sure.' Mrs Blythe took a note out of the till. 'Here.'

'I canna take that.'

Mrs Blythe came out from behind the counter, encouraging Tommy toward the door.

'We'll call it an advance on your wages. There's a kiddie to consider now. What either of you want doesn't come into it. Tidy yourself up a bit, take her some flowers, tell her you're earning.' She took his jacket by the lapels and shook it into position.

'What if she'll not 'ave us?'

'Then she's dafter than I thought. Decent lad like you, she could do a lot worse.'

'Thanks Mrs B. I won't let her down.'

'Now you see as you don't. Billy Barker'll stand by you if you do right by his daughter. You're only kids yourselves. That missus of his raised six o' them. She'll know a thing or two.'

'I luv her.' He looked at the note in his hand. She came round and stood beside him.

'Loves got nothing to do with it. You got what you were after, and you were unlucky.' Mrs Blythe put her hand on his shoulder. 'Things need taking care of even if the horse has bolted. Let's get you wed and some money in your pocket to keep a roof over the child's head, clothes on its back and food in its belly.'

'And ours.'

'Yes, well, that goes without saying. The child comes first.'

''Course.'

'Now be off with you, and get the girl a ring, best you can afford.' She encouraged him out the door.

Tommy looked at the floor.

Mrs Blythe went behind the counter and took more notes out of the till.

'Here, we'll call it a bonus.'

'You've give us enough already.'

'Nonsense.'

Tommy put the money in his wallet.

'I'll expect you at eight sharp on Monday morning. No need for the suit. Decent trousers and shirt should do it.

Jackets get in the way.' She opened the door.

'Thanks, Mrs B.'

'Oh and Tommy …'

'Yes?'

'Congratulations.'

Surprise Discovery

My mam is moving to an apartment. Overwhelmed with the task of sorting decades of belongings, she has requested my help.

The drawer in my mam's sideboard gives off a faint aroma of roses. It sticks on its runners, and it takes several goes to free it from its position. It jerks, and papers, paperclips, broken brooches, and other detritus tumble out.

I bend to retrieve the contents from the floor and spot a bundle of opened letters. My name is written on the top envelope by a vaguely familiar hand. When I remove the elastic band, I find they are all addressed to me. I wonder who they are from.

I open one. It's from Sarah, a girl I dated years ago. I can't recall her writing to me. Someone — it must have been me — has opened these letters — I must have read them. I stuff the envelopes in my rucksack and carry on clearing the sideboard drawers.

Concentration is difficult. My mind drifts to Sarah and our time together.

'Matt, we deserve a break.' Mam's voice interrupts my thoughts.

A tray of tea and homemade cake arrives beside me, making my stomach rumble.

'Thanks, Mam.' A welcome break, despite the drag to reality.

***

Afterward, driven by nostalgia, I climb into my loft at home to find the photo album from the year I dated Sarah. After a long root through various boxes and a few diversions down memory lane I find the album I'm looking for. There's one photo of my camera-shy girlfriend which I remove. I like the idea of having her with me, in a sense, as I read her letters. The year we spent together as volunteers changed our lives.

She took a lot of photos. The images capture moments of our experiences together. I am in a few of them. We both wanted reminders of the people we met. We thought we would look at the photos together one day, maybe revisit the place we first met. The letters have made me want to see her face again.

I make my way down the loft ladder to the sitting room and sit in my favourite chair with her photo and the letters, ready to delve into the past.

I open one at random.

"The Matt I knew was better than this. I can't do this alone. It's too much. I have to give her up for her sake."

What? Who?

I reach for another, hoping for answers.

"I hoped we could do this together. I know we agreed no contact, my pregnancy changes things."

Pregnant? Sarah was pregnant?

I head to my liquor cabinet. News like this need's whiskey. I take a sip before opening the third letter. When I do, a photo of a baby falls out. Baby? I read the letter.

"I can't do this on my own. Look — this is your daughter; her name is Jayne. You haven't replied to my letters. I thought a photograph might prick your conscience."

I drop the letter to my lap. My head whirls. I want to be sick; my heart pounds and I'm gasping for air. I rub my eyes and read the paragraph again. Tears fill my eyes.

I am a father.

This wasn't how I expected to be told I'd fathered a child. In my dreams, I would be with the mother. We would go through the pregnancy together, take home our tiny human, fuss too much, get no sleep and take endless photos and …

I have a daughter. I check the date on the envelope.

A twenty-two-year-old daughter.

I sip my whiskey, take a few deep breaths, pace the floor, my mind racing. My splayed fingers alternately run through my hair and cover my face.

There's only one answer. My mam opened these letters, read them, and kept them.

I need to know the full story before I decide what to do. I've been kept in the dark long enough.

I try to be calm. Reading the letters evokes a range of emotions rampaging through my veins. My hands can't stem the flow of my tears, forcing me to stop reading several times. The crushing pain in my chest is so strong I have to tell myself it's not a heart attack. My pounding head leads me to break for painkillers. As I sip on water to fight the nausea, I put the story together.

"Matt, I'm pregnant. The baby's due in June. Will you contact me please? We need to discuss it. I've tried calling. Have you changed your number? The line goes dead?"

The three I opened come after that.

There's joy bubbling in the confusion. Grief at the wasted years, tinged with curiosity. My daughter is a stranger, a grown woman. I never expected to be an absent father, just a name on a piece of paper. My child grew up without me. I want to know everything about her, to have her in my life, if she is willing.

I pace. My clenched fists need a target to release the pain. Given my anger is directed at my mam, I can't hit the source.

My need for answers makes me want to storm round there and have it out with her. I walk to the car before I come to my senses. Nothing will be achieved by dragging her out of bed in the middle of the night. If I want a sensible conversation, I have to wait till morning. I can't process any information she has, even if she is capable of rational thought at this hour.

The following morning, I can't eat. I bolt my coffee and head to my mam's.

I ring the bell, hopping from foot to foot, my head spinning in disbelief. She answers. I stride past her and head into the kitchen which smells of toast and last night's fish and chips.

'Matt, are you ok? What's going on? Do you want a slice of toast?' She adjusts her dressing gown, munches on her toast, and touches my arm.

I knock her hand off. She jerks away, her mouth agape.

'No, I am not ok. What right have you to open my mail?' I slam the letters on the table. 'Were you ever going to tell me?'

She gasps and attempts to grab them. I snatch them and return them to my pocket. I can't risk losing them.

I haven't been able to look at her, although I need to see her face, to see if she feels any regret or acknowledgement of the pain she has caused me. She has to understand how her actions hurt me if we are to save our relationship.

I'm imprisoned in this kitchen. I want to run. I chose to come here. Why did she keep the letters from me? She loves me. Loving someone means not hurting them. I'm being torn apart, little shreds of my former existence falling from me at this unexpected fakery.

She swallows, her frown lines pronounced as she regards me with her brown eyes. An edge of uncertainty cracks my anger. Can I do this to my ageing mother? The smell of toast almost makes me buckle.

'I did what I thought was best at the time. You were young; you weren't ready to be a dad. Girls try to trap boys claiming to be pregnant, looking for a free ride. It wasn't until the last letter I considered she might be telling the truth.'

Her attempt at justification leaves me cold. I tower over her. She shivers in the face of my anger.

'How dare you! I was twenty-two, not sixteen. A man — not your little boy. It was my choice to make, not yours. You've had twenty-two years to tell me. Twenty-two years!'

I show her Jayne's baby photo and continue with my rant.

'I have a daughter out there. Your granddaughter. Does that mean anything to you? The fact we couldn't have kids broke my marriage. It almost destroyed me. Did you not consider it would have been better being told at the time than finding out like this?'

She's crying as I stomp across the kitchen.

'I'm sorry.' She gulps. 'The child was adopted; it was too late.'

She stands, hitting the table. 'It was better you didn't know than go through the pain of knowing she was out there somewhere, and she wasn't in your life!'

I storm back and forth in front of her as if she is in the dock and I am cross-examining her.

'Sorry? It's way too late for sorry, don't you think? And her name's Jayne. At least it was. I have no idea what it is now.'

She keeps her eyes on me. Fury rises inside me threatening to explode. The more she tries to defend her actions the harder it is to remind myself of her vulnerability.

'What are you going to do? Can I help?'

Out of the corner of my eye I catch her fingering the photograph.

'I've no idea. You've done more than enough already. Let me do this my way.'

I take the photo from her and stamp to the door.

'Matt, please don't go like this. I love you.'

She follows me, grabbing at me, trying to stop me leaving. I squirm to avoid her grip.

'I love you too Mam. I'm just not sure I like you at the moment,' I say in her vague direction.

I leave before I say any more. I'm shaking.

***

When I get home, I try to process the swirl of emotions running through me and work out what I can do.

Sadness fills my heart for Jayne, for Sarah, and for myself. Sarah needed me and I wasn't there for her. Our daughter might have grown up with her birth parents if we'd been given the choice.

I don't know what I would have done. Sarah wanted to travel the world while I preferred to make a difference close to home. The idea of a long-term relationship wasn't an option we discussed. We could have been a family. Our daughter's arrival into the world would have changed things.

I can't change the past …

I can't let my child go, now I know about her, without a fight.

I have an approximate birth date, and a possible birthplace for Jayne. It's not enough.

I could try to find Sarah. I have no phone number and after all this time she may not want to know.

The address is old. Given her aspirations for travel she could be anywhere. Her parents might still live there. I could show Sarah's photo to people and find out if anyone knows her whereabouts if the address is no help.

Our daughter is out there somewhere, and neither Jayne nor Sarah know I care because of my interfering mother. I'm doubled over in pain, tears flowing onto the carpet.

Sarah could be in a relationship; she could have more children.

If Jayne was adopted, the parents could have changed her name.

I hope if I find Sarah she will understand, because without her I have no chance of finding Jayne.

I don't know what shocks me more — finding out I have a twenty-two-year-old daughter I knew nothing about or the fact my mother hid it from me. Dealing with my mother will have to wait; I have to focus on Sarah.

I suppose it's too much to expect she changed her mind and raised Jayne herself. The Sarah I remember was strong. She could do anything. Her letters said she couldn't manage alone. I have to know what happened. The internet gives me no help other than directions.

I message my mam. No matter how mad I am, I can't just disappear.

'Going to look for Sarah, booked a week off work.'

The reply comes.
'I hope you find her. Love you.'

We need time apart. I can't reconcile this behaviour with the woman who raised me. I've no idea where our relationship goes from here.

I put Sarah's photo in my wallet in case her parents have moved. Perhaps someone will recognise her and be able to help.

I toss a hastily packed bag of clothes and toiletries into the boot. I add a few bits and pieces I've thrown together including the photo album and the letters. My stomach is in knots and my heart is racing. I owe it to Sarah to try to fix this. I have no idea what will happen if and when I find her. Jayne is my daughter. I haven't been allowed to be a father to her in any sense of the word. I'm prepared to do whatever it takes to be part of her life.

I ring the number I found for Sarah's parents. I have practised what to say if they answer. I hope that if I find them, they will accept my story and help me.

A lump forms in my throat when an unfamiliar female voice answers the phone …

First Night Alone

It's 9:30 pm. The store closes at 10 pm. Jack wrestles his screaming daughter into her car seat, both of them covered in the last of the formula. He turns the key in the ignition. Zero response.

He wiggles his phone out of his pocket and calls a taxi.

'It'll be fifteen minutes.'

Ava continues screaming. He blocks one ear with his hand.

'Sssh, it's OK.'

'Oooohh, I'll tell them to rush.'

Jack removes Ava from her car seat and is set upon by flailing limbs for his trouble. He paces with Ava clamped to his soaked shirt.

The taxi arrives at the store at 9:55 pm. He scoops Ava into his arms and runs to get formula.

***

Mandy comes home at 11 pm. Ava's asleep. Jack is sprawled on the sofa in a clean t-shirt.

'Any problems, Jack?'

'Nothing to report.' He flicks channels with the remote, stifling a yawn.

'I might go out more often.' Mandy smiles and goes upstairs.

Jack slumps on the sofa, his head in his hands.

My Angel

Dressed as a fairy she ran into the melee, her face a picture of delight.

I shut my eyes and crossed my fingers. Stealing glances, I drank my coffee and read my book.

The play centre was packed to bursting with toys and every pre-schooler within a ten-mile radius. Angelica played with them all.

Eyes narrowed. Hands on hips. Teeth bared. Destruction was coming. I bribed her with juice and biscuits. Filled with sugar, she rampaged, grabbing toys from crying children.

The parents may not have appreciated me ignoring it. My bank balance was struggling to cope. My mini wrecking ball had earned me top supporter status. I'd replaced half the toys in the place at my own expense.

I swept her into my arms while she kicked, punched, and screamed her desire for freedom. Another Wednesday effort to get her socialised for school.

Sandcastles

The 2023 sandcastle competition attracted some outstanding entries.

Alastair Cowan, the pretender to tech giant AMCO's throne had used all his skills to design his entry in minute detail.

Lizzie Smith, the building giant's granddaughter, had worked out the exact ratios of sand to water for the construction.

The meteorologist Bill Withernsea had studied the weather conditions to make sure the structure held for the required time.

Six-year-old Jenny Schubert had her bucket and spade, chopsticks, and enthusiasm.

Storm Chasers

The steely tinges in the sky, present since dawn, blanketed the town. The wind raged through the streets. Trees swayed and broke, sending branch missiles hurtling in unexpected directions.

Mac was out in this weather. While he considered himself invincible, Ruby didn't agree with her seventeen-year-old son. The memories of loss at the hands of previous storms added to her worry. She wasn't going to let him be the latest sacrifice.

***

Ruby and Chris had been storm chasers. With their group of friends, they spent their teenage years daring each other to be the closest to the eye of the storm. Ruby and Ellie, Ruby's best friend, stopped when they became parents, the others carried on.

One night they took it too far.

'Chris, grow up. It's dangerous out there.' She glared at him from her losing tussle against seven-year-old Mac for the dining table. She was trying to set it for dinner as he filled it with Lego.

Chris shoved his arms into his coat and snatched his keys. 'It's my life, not yours. You've gotten so boring. I'm going to live!'

'Someone has to be responsible.' Ruby pulled him away from the door, her heart doubling its pace. 'We have a child to consider. Please, Chris.'

'I want Mac to be proud of his old man.' He puffed out his chest.

'He will be, without you risking your life to prove whatever you're trying to prove.' Ruby lashed out, hitting him.

Chris restrained her and took hold of her shoulders. 'Try to understand, Ruby, I have to do this. This will be the last time. I love you.' He kissed her.

'Love you too,' she managed before he was gone.

It was the last time. Chris and his friends never came home. Seven-year-old Mac lost his dad.

***

Mac reminded Ruby of Chris. She was damned if she would lose him too.

She phoned her friend. 'Ellie, you've got to help me. Mac's storm chasing. We have to find him.' Ruby's stomach churned and tears came to her eyes.

'Hold on, I'm coming.'

Within minutes Ellie and Ruby were in Ellie's car scouring the neighbourhood. Tree branches littered the road, fences threatening to join them. Ellie strained to see through the rivers of rain on her windscreen. She battled the wind playing ping pong with the car.

Every time they saw a kid on a bike, Ruby opened the window.

'Go home, it's not safe!' she screamed into the night.

They ignored her.

The rain bounced off the ground. Sodden missiles of rubbish flew past the windows while Ruby made a frantic search for Mac. Once or twice she thought she spotted him. The neon flashes turned out to be workers fighting to get home.

Finally, she spotted Mac cycling with a gang of youths heading over the bridge.

'Ellie, there!' Ruby shouted above the drumming on the car roof.

'Don't worry, I'll catch them,' Ellie shouted back.

She put her foot down, spun the car round and blocked the bridge.

Mac screeched to a halt before he hit the car. He threw his arms in the air and rolled his eyes.

'What the …?'

His friends formed a cluster behind him.

'Get in,' Ruby ordered.

His friends laughed.

'Mammy come to get you?'

'You out past your bedtime, naughty boy?'

Mac scowled at his friends, flushing scarlet.

'Mum, stop being embarrassing. We're nearly there.' He pointed with both hands at the rolling storm clouds.

'That's what I'm afraid of. You getting in or do we have to force you?'

'Put the bike in the boot, Mac.' Ellie stood beside Ruby.

'You know what happened to your dad.' Ruby took hold of his shoulders. 'Please. I can't go through it again with you.'

'It won't happen to me.'

'That's what he said.'

'Mac, come on, don't do this.' Ellie took hold of Mac's bike.

‘OK. Sorry guys, gotta go.’ Mac pulled a face at his waiting friends and with all the reluctance of a thwarted teenager, put the bike in the boot. He wrenched open the back door and slouched in the seat.

‘Go home. It’s not safe,’ Ruby told his friends.

They shared raised eyebrows and rode off toward the storm. Roof tiles flew past them on their path between uprooted trees.

***

The following morning Mac found Ruby crying in the kitchen. When she saw him, she gave him a hug.

'Mum, what's the matter?'

She put the newspaper in his hand. A collage of photos of his friends filled the front page.

The headline read: '*They never came home.*'

Unending

It's in the Cards

'I am with you always.'

The inscription on the locket from her grandmother filled her with a warm glow and brought a tear to her eye. She tied her planets and stars scarf around her head and checked in the mirror. Madame Alithea smiled back at her.

Her booth was busy all evening with serious people alone or with a friend and with giggling groups daring each other to have a reading.

***

The coffee shop was empty when April arrived at the end of the day. Her smile grew wider with every blank space on the wall.

Rob, the café owner, saw her from the steaming coffee machine. His smile matched April's.

'When you bringing more paintings?' he asked.

'Tomorrow?' April stuttered.

'Yeah, great. People love your art, and the way it sells, you can knock the Madame Alithea stuff on the head soon.'

Rob stopped clearing tables and came over to April with a fresh cup of coffee.

'It's a long way off, if it happens at all.' April sipped her coffee and took in the familiarity of the café. She loved sitting here at this time of day. It was a quiet space to pause and reflect before she made her way home.

Rob shook his head.

'I love being Madame Alithea,' April said. 'Using my grandmother's cards helps me keep a sense of connection to her.' She fingered her locket.

'I believe in you, April Stevens. Your grandmother did too. You're an artist; it's your calling.'

April collected her belongings and walked home with Rob's words ringing in her ears.

***

The following day, April watched a customer approach. The business-suited woman carried a briefcase that resembled April's bank manager's. Her stomach knotted. This didn't look like her usual client.

'Hi, I'm Sonya Taylor.' The woman held out her card. 'Taylor's Art Gallery.'

The knot in April's stomach tightened.

'Madame Alithea. How can I help?' April shuffled her cards.

'I know who you are. You're April Stevens. I bought one of your pieces from the café. The owner gave me your name and told me where to find you. Would you consider having an event at my gallery?'

April's mouth dropped open.

'Me? Really? Are you sure?'

'I'm sure. I visit the café often. I've seen a lot of your work. You have talent. I know people would be interested.' Sonya put a gallery brochure on the table. 'What do you think?'

April flicked through the brochure. 'Thank you, I would love to.'

'I'll be in touch.' Sonya shook April's hand.

She kept hold of Sonya's hand. 'Which piece did you buy?'

'It's a house. It belonged to a woman I knew. A tarot reader like you.'

April's grandmother's house.

She wrapped her locket in her hand and mouthed a 'thank you' to the sky.

'I am with you always.'

A Shock to the System

Elizabeth moved into sheltered housing at short notice when her mobility required she leave the family residence. Her son Charles had been tasked to deal with the house and the belongings left behind while his sister Judy took care of their mother's needs.

Amongst his mother's possessions, Charles found several books by someone called Diana Munroe set aside from the rest. The cover of one attracted his attention; the view from his grandmother's porch.

Charles' mother Elizabeth Perkins carried her camera everywhere and a photo of the same scene hung in her study.

According to the blurb on the back of the book, the characters Peter and Wendy were writers.

Charles opened the book at random.

"Peter entered his study laden with fruit and ice cream. Wendy lay across his desk. Hunger filled his body. He longed to feast on the naked banquet."

'Ugh!'

Charles' latex-clad hands removed the offending books from the shelf and flung them into a box. One opened at the "About the Author" page and Charles' eyes met with a photo of his mother.

His sister Judy found him on the floor.

***

Charles watched from his bed when Judy wheeled their mother into the ward. The clinical whiteness of the place matched his exacting standards. Judy noted the scrubbed white walls, the sparkling silver grey floor tiles, and the gleaming chrome. There was not a fingerprint in sight.

Machines attached to Charles beeped a welcome. Charles fought to raise himself in greeting.

'Mother, what on earth?'

Judy parked the wheelchair and took her brother's hands. She fought the urge to smile.

'I knew you should have told him. He might have enjoyed reading your books.'

Elizabeth hit her arm.

'Your brother is not as open-minded as you.'

'You knew and never told me.' He pumped his sister's arms.

Judy released his hands and walked to the window.

Elizabeth straightened herself in her wheelchair.

'I had to have a hobby, Charles. Your father enjoyed acting out scenes with me. It did wonders for our sex life.'

'Oh, my God! Mother!' Charles covered his ears.

The machine's waltz-like beep escalated into a samba.

Judy's shoulders shook.

'For goodness' sake, grow up! Your father and I had a healthy sex life. It's nothing to be ashamed of.'

'But he died five years ago, and your last book was …'

He shut his eyes and ran his hands across his face.

'Last year, yes. My friend Tom was most obliging in that department.' Elizabeth smirked.

'You're too old for all that business.'

The machine's beeps became a jive.

'A woman has needs, even at my age. We're not all as buttoned up as you. No wonder you're alone if the idea of people having sex does this to you!' She fussed with her clothes.

The dance-like beeping turned to screeching. A nurse ran into the room, followed by a team.

Judy and Elizabeth held each other.

A blur of coloured uniforms obscured their view.

The noise descended into silence.

'I'm sorry for your loss, Mrs Perkins.'

‘Oh, being dead will suit him.’ She put her hand on the male doctor’s arm. ‘He always was such a stiff.’

Lost

Doreen reached for the dresser as she stumbled, sending her father's photo skidding across the polished wood, and smashing to the floor. She landed in a heap on the sofa and burst into tears.

'Not again! It can't be happening again. Another child in this family losing their dad.'

Her daughter Celia sat beside her and held her in her arms.

'My Lucy will be ok.' Celia kissed her mother. 'She has us. We'll help her raise Thomas. We know how difficult it is, raising a child alone.'

Doreen sobbed on her shoulder.

'And growing up without a father. Senseless violence. Eighty years, eighty bloody years, and we've learnt nothing.' Doreen dabbed her eyes with her handkerchief.

'I know, it's horrible.' Celia poured two cups of tea.

'I was only two.' Doreen screwed up her fists. 'I have no memory of my dad, thanks to Hitler. Just a damn photo! The Falklands took your dad, my poor Robert, and then you lost your Alfie. So unfair for you to lose a father and a husband the way you did.'

'At least Lucy remembers her dad.' Celia twisted her wedding ring round her finger.

'Fifteen was still too young for Lucy to lose her dad.' Doreen heaved herself off the sofa, bent and returned the remains of her father's photo to the dresser.

'So is six. Thomas is the same age I was when I lost my dad.' Celia nibbled her biscuit.

'When you marry a soldier or a firefighter, you know there's a risk. This was a stupid idiot with a knife! Matt died because he was there. He didn't do anything; he was just in the wrong place at the wrong time. He went out for groceries for heaven's sake! Is even that not safe now?'

Doreen bashed the cushions against each other and shook them into shape.

'Kids losing their fathers because someone is angry. We all get angry. We don't all kill people.' Celia tided the magazines on the table with trembling fingers.

Doreen paced the sitting room carpet.

'My father thought he was fighting for freedom,' she turned to face her daughter. 'To keep us all safe. Your dad was protecting people. Alfie was saving people. Matt only wanted to feed his son.'

She sat for a few seconds, drumming her fingers on the chair arm before resuming her pacing.

'None of them needed to die so bloody young. Matt didn't sign up to put himself in danger. He was a youth worker trying to help kids like the one who put a knife in him. My grandson has to grow up without a dad because his dad went to buy him food. This has to stop!'

Celia hugged her mother.

'This is another kind of war. One no-one signed up for.'

Two Minute Silence

They'd cancelled the Remembrance Day parade. Jack decided to spend the two minute silence at his great-grandfather's grave. When he arrived at the cemetery, it was empty save a lone figure in the distance.

Jack shielded his eyes from the sun hitting the white gravestones. He navigated the path worn through the grass by countless feet to his great-grandfather's grave, right next to the grave where the stranger was standing. On it lay a red silk poppy wreath, like the one Jack carried.

'Who are you visiting?' the stranger asked.

'My great-grandfather. I was named after him. I'm Jack.' Jack laid his wreath on the grave.

'Same here. I'm Charlie.'

Jack shook Charlie's hand with his firm, strong grip.

'They served in the same regiment,' Jack observed, peering at the gravestone Charlie stood beside.

'They might have known each other.' Charlie brushed the headstone.

'Yeah, they might have.' Jack gave Charlie a quick smile. 'I wanted to do something when we couldn't have the parade.'

'Me too. What time is it?' Charlie patted his pockets and pulled out his phone.

Jack looked at his phone. The programme playing on silent switched to the memorial service at the cenotaph.

'It's time.' He adjusted the volume to help them synchronise their timing for the two minute silence.

They stood to attention, facing the rows of countless white tombstones providing one last parade. The scent of the flowers on nearby graves gave a pleasant aroma.

After the silence, they exchanged smiles and Charlie prepared to leave.

'It's sad they died so young. Such a waste.' Jack's gaze covered the cemetery.

'My grandfather hardly knew his dad. He was still at school when he died.' Charlie sighed.

'If they met, what would they have done?' Jack stroked his great-grandfather's gravestone.

Charlie shuffled, his eyes on the ground. 'Shared a pint, I guess.' He looked at his great-grandfather's grave.

'How about we raise a glass to them?'

'Sounds good.' Charlie bowed his head.

'You coming? I'm buying.' Jack indicated the gate of the cemetery with his head.

'OK, thanks.' Charlie glanced at the graves, then followed Jack.

They made their way out of the cemetery together.

The pub heaved with people in uniform who welcomed the young men wearing their great-grandfather's medals.

Till Death Us Do Part

And he spoke of the length of the days like he hadn't considered them before. As if the thought just occurred to him. The sun being high in the sky when he woke and low as he considered his evening meal. The seasons changing. The daylight hours fluctuating. The clothing he plucked from his closet becoming slowly unsuitable, requiring adjustment to ensure his temperature remained on a somewhat even keel.

The days away from her mounted up. Too many to count now. He was at once glad she wasn't here to see this and sad she wasn't by his side. The photographs were a poor substitute for her physical presence. Better the daily reminder than the sorrow of her being almost erased from his life as if their past had never happened.

His love for her would accompany him to the end of his days. Her love for him her legacy.

Unexplained

Bridge Echoes

The girl appeared, dripping wet, on the path in front of me. I found it unusual to see a girl in a dress; my kids lived in shorts or trousers. I skidded as I tried to brake to avoid hitting her. I climbed off my bike and leaned it against the nearest tree, my feet sliding on the wet leaves.

Where had she come from? I shivered from the cold despite the sunshine. Mist drifted along the path snaking round her. Silence replaced the birdsong and burbling river of a few seconds ago. The light breeze making the temperature bearable drifted away.

'Sir, don't go there. It's not safe.' The girl half-turned, her dripping hand pointed toward the town.

I followed her gaze.

Shielding my eyes with my hand, I could see the bridge was out.

'Wow, where's the bridge? What happened to you?'

'Fell in, didn't I.' She looked at the ground.

'Are you hurt?' I ran my eyes over her parentally, looking for injury.

'No, sir. Don't you go worrying about me. My momma will take care of me.'

'OK, go and get warm. You'll catch your death hanging around like that.'

'Will do, sir.' She made a little bob.

'Where's your momma?'

'Back there, sir.' Her arm stretched out behind her.

'Right you go find her. Thanks for the warning about the bridge.'

'Thank you, sir.' She bobbed again.

As I turned my bike around, the warmth returned to my bones. I looked behind me to check where the girl had gone. She'd disappeared. I got on my bike and cycled along the path. The lapping river accompanied my journey home.

My encounter nagged at me. *Who was she? Where was her mother? What happened?*

***

Late that evening while reading the local paper, I came across this:

One Hundred Years Ago
2nd September 1921
Bridge Collapse Fatalities

An unfortunate incident occurred at Longdale yesterday resulting in the death of Mrs. George Thomas, wife of Mr. George Thomas of Willow Green, together with their daughter Miss. G Thomas, 10 years of age.

Mr. Albert Jackson lost control of his barge, which he was using to ferry goods to Storley. The vehicle collided with the Albertine bridge, causing its collapse. Mrs. Thomas and her daughter were travelling into town on foot via the structure. They were cast into the Jubilee and caught in its current. Onlookers reported screaming before silence informed them of the victims' untimely demise. The bodies were recovered this morning.

We extend our deepest condolences to Mr. Thomas, a well-respected gentleman of his parish.

Jackson has been called to answer to the court Monday next to account for his actions.

The following day, I cycled along the river path to check on the bridge. It was intact.

Power

The boy squinted at the house, concentrating on the tiled roof, the neat windows, and the pale stonework. The house shifted to the right.

He needed to try harder. Concentrate. Focus. This time it moved a few feet to the left.

Could he put it back?

Yes! The house stood exactly as before. Even the cat on the windowsill seemed undisturbed.

He blinked and rubbed his eyes.

He set his phone to record.

He raised his arms above his head straight to the sky, and in a fluid movement brought them down to his sides.

He bent his knees and jumped, twirling his arms as he did and landed facing the opposite direction.

He checked. The house did too!

One last push. He shook himself and got into position.

He jumped and twirled all the way round.

He hit play on his phone to check what happened.

Success!

He punched the air.

He couldn't wait till there were people inside.

The Stranger on the Bridge

I met him on the bridge at sunset, which sounds romantic —strangers meeting by chance in a beautiful location …

Trust me, it wasn't.

Walking across the bridge helps me clear my head. The workers have gone for the day and the nightlife hasn't kicked in yet; so I tend to have the place to myself. I love to watch the lights illuminate the city. It's peaceful on the bridge, watching the city shift from day to night.

A figure appeared out of the darkness of the park. Dressed in black from head to toe, he joined me on the bridge. The paleness of his face coming toward me attracted my attention.

He stopped in front of me, I moved to let him pass. He mirrored my movement.

He carried a box. The careful way he cradled it suggested the contents to be fragile or valuable, or both. He offered it to me.

I made no move to take it.

He took a step closer and gave the box a gentle shove against my chest.

Under the watch of his mesmerising dark eyes, resistance was futile. My hands reached for the box. Its lightness took me by surprise.

'Hey, what are you doing?' I held it out to him.

He crossed his arms and glared at me.

'What is it?'

He put his finger to his lips to shush me as you would a child.

'Why are you giving it to me?'

He didn't reply.

'What do you want me to do with it?'

His silence added to my curiosity.

The darkness swallowed him. He disappeared, leaving an evaporating mist in his wake. I shouted after him, to no effect.
I rubbed my eyes and spun round, looking in every direction. The park was deserted. He was gone.

I shivered. What just happened? If it weren't for the box in my hands, I would have thought I was dreaming.

The square brown paper package was addressed to a doctor at the local hospital.

What was it? Who was he? Why did he give it to me? I could have kept it, whatever it was. Did he trust me, a stranger he met on a bridge, to deliver it for him? Why didn't he take it himself?

The hospital wasn't far. I didn't know what else to do with the package, so I walked down dark streets to take it there.

***

Temporarily blinded by the glare of the fluorescent lights in the hospital foyer, I found the reception desk. The familiarity of the arrival routine, gained from many hospital experiences offered a little comfort despite the unusual circumstances of my visit. With no noticeable reaction, the receptionist put in a call and told me to wait.

It occurred to me there could be a bomb in the box. There was no ticking sound. I didn't think there was anything to worry about — not that I was any expert.

The warning signs about unattended packages at every tube stop replayed in my head. My sweaty palms struggled to keep hold of the box as a nauseous lump rose in my throat.

After a few minutes, a doctor appeared. Her name tag matched the name on the box. I took a deep breath. I hoped she would take this mysterious package from me.

'Hi,' I smiled. 'I met a man on the bridge in the park.' I cleared my throat. 'He gave me this. I've no idea what's in it. It's not heavy. It might be fragile.'

When she returned my smile, her eyes deepened into a shade reminiscent of the man on the bridge. They shared the same pale complexion as if darkness was an eternal companion.

'Thank you,' she said. 'I appreciate you bringing it to me.'

'It's no trouble.'

Her smile remained intact as her hands relieved me of the package. I was reluctant to transfer ownership. I stood there, grinning. My curiosity grew stronger. I wanted to know what was inside the box.

She opened it and put her hand inside, checking to make sure the contents remained intact. Her fingers revealed nothing.

She looked at me, hunger in her eyes. 'Thank you.'

The Man in Black

In the town of Halloween, there is a twilight that exists nowhere else: it's the light of a thousand candles against the October sky. The town's eerie emptiness is taken over during the celebration of Halloween. Abandoned buildings pay homage to its last inhabitants.

My visit is engraved on my memory.

In a rowdy crowd of drinking revellers gorging on delights from the table in the barn, he stood alone. He was dressed in black, his cape flapping in the icy wind. The mask over his face left his eyes and mouth exposed. His voice was liquid chocolate. He rationed its use.

Julia downed her vodka in one. 'I'm going over.' She braced herself.

I grabbed her arm. 'I don't think that's a good idea.'

'Jay, he's fascinating. A quiet masked man. He's the stuff of fantasies.' She tilted her head toward the sky, closed her eyes and licked her lips.

'Yours, maybe. Can't see the appeal myself. Creepy.' I shuddered.

She darted me a quick raise of her eyebrows and sauntered over to the man. He reached out to touch her.

A chill of unease crept through my body.

A group of revellers knocked into me, making me fall on my knees. By the time I righted myself, she'd disappeared. The man stood alone.

My stomach rose into my throat. I looked for her, running from place to place. It was a one-road town, my search didn't take long. The buildings stood empty, and the usual occupants of the cars lining the pavement would be at the party. Traffic did not pass this way. Halloween was the end of the road. Julia was nowhere to be found.

When I returned to the barn fifteen minutes later, I found it empty, the tables cleared, and chairs stacked. Music floated in the air. The man in black stood outside.

Aliens for hire

In a portacabin off the motorway, a shivering receptionist turned the electric heater on and put his takeaway coffee on the cluttered desk by the window. The bare grey walls reflected his mood. The phone's annoying tones filled the silence before the computer came to life. Huddled in his coat, the receptionist tried to force a smile. He scrambled for a pen to write in the battered diary and answered the telephone.

'Good morning, Aliens 'R' Us.'

Silence.

Clunk. He returned the phone to its cradle.

A few seconds later, the tuneless music returned.

'Good morning, Aliens 'R' Us … Yes, we have a range of Aliens you can hire by the hour.' He paused. 'No, they don't attack or kill.'

He sighed and sipped his coffee.

'Good morning, Aliens 'R' Us … We're not that kind of agency, perhaps a dating app …'

He scrolled social media and ended the call.

'Good morning, Aliens 'R' Us … Yes, you have to be over eighteen to hire an Alien.'

The receptionist yawned.

'Good morning, Aliens 'R' Us … Yes, the prices on our website are correct.'

He nibbled his biscuit.

'Good morning, Aliens 'R' Us … Yes, we expect them returned alive and in the same condition in which they came to you.’

His feet covered the small space in seconds as he paced.

‘Good morning, Aliens ‘R’ Us … We have three packages, Bronze, Silver, and Gold … You do have to complete an Alien Awareness course and have a qualification in Alien care.’

He checked his emails.

‘Good morning, Aliens ‘R’ Us … No, sorry, we’re fully booked this month. You could try Instant Alien …’

He clicked round the website, making his routine checks.

‘Good morning, Aliens ‘R’ Us … Bronze is decorative purposes only. They have no skills. Great for selfies though …’

He pulled a range of expressions for his phone camera.

‘Good morning, Aliens ‘R’ Us …
Silver? Silver can do simple tasks. Serve food and drink, take coats, that sort of thing …’

He shrugged his coat off.

‘Good morning, Aliens ‘R’ Us …
Gold? Gold can mingle with your guests. They have basic conversational English …’

He opened the booking form. The line went dead.

‘Good morning, Aliens ‘R’ Us.’

Heavy breathing.

He ended the call.

‘Good morning, Aliens ‘R’ Us …
There's no need to be abusive.'

He slammed the phone down.

'Good morning, Aliens 'R' Us … Yes, we can take bookings for Christmas. You need to complete your Alien Awareness course and have your certificate in Alien Care before the event … You have already, great. Can I take a few details?'

The receptionist opened the booking form on the computer. 'The manager isn't available at the moment … The police, right. Where will your event be held? Oh, you don't want to make a booking? … Alien trafficking you say?'

He grabbed his coat and bag.

'No, I didn't know … Yes, of course I will let the manager know … My name?'

He laid the handset on the desk and left the portacabin.

The House of Justice

Moon kept an all-night vigil on the House of Justice. The grey building was full to bursting for this landmark case.

Justice was weary. The evidence had taken months to wade through and the witness list could paper the walls.

The Planets were taking People to court for their abuse of Earth.

'What happened while I was asleep?' Sun looked into his friend Moon's sad face.

Moon got to her feet, stretched, and drained the remains of her thermos into her mug.

'They're still in there. This has tested Justice to their limits.'

Sun took his friend's vacated seat, placing his provisions bag between his legs.

***

Earth sat in the gallery yawning.

Venus put her arm round her. 'You should get some rest.'

'Mars is next; he will want to destroy People. He wants them to suffer for this.' Earth slumped forward.

'You're beaten up. We left you in their care and they abused our trust.' She passed Earth a mug of hot chocolate.

'I'm ok. This is too much. If the ruling goes in my favour, it's The Complete Chaos punishment. People don't deserve that.' She hung her head. 'Hurricanes, tornados, earthquakes, firestorms, ice storms, volcanic eruptions, coastal erosion … I can't …' She ran her hands down her legs.

'Justice is fair. They want all sides of the story. Hopefully that won't be necessary.'

'You will speak up for them, won't you?' Earth turned to face Venus.

'Of course. I think Justice will put the army on double time, throw every bit of minor punishment at them in rotation. Rain, Sleet, Hail, and Snow are ready. Wind and her family are in training already. Sun has agreed to join in if that's what Justice decides.'

'People won't be happy about that.' Earth rubbed her eyes.

'Moon will be in charge and make sure they don't get out of control.' Venus ran her fingers through her hair.

Moon came into the gallery.

'Earth, come and sit in my fishing boat on the Sea of Tranquillity till Justice makes a ruling. Sun will let us know what happens before he goes to bed.' Moon held Earth's hands.

'Why don't you take up her offer?' Venus encouraged. 'It's not good for you to listen to this.'

Earth hugged them both.

'Try not to worry. They need a few sanctions to protect you, let them know we mean business.' Venus guided Earth to the door.

***

Sun called in on Moon on his way to bed.

Moon was writing a note to Earth when she woke in the fishing boat.

'Has Justice arrived at a decision?'

'As we expected,' Moon told Earth. 'Double shifts for the army in rotation, keep them under twenty-four-hour surveillance with rotating minor consequences and heavy penalties for any misbehaviour. Justice is keeping the situation under review. The Complete Chaos punishment with free-for-all is not out of the question in the future.'

Earth raised herself into a sitting position.

'What did People say?'

'They showed remorse. They're training to improve their performance. They have goals to complete and further sanctions if they fail. I think their acceptance of the situation tempered Justice's response for now.'

Earth hugged her.

'Let's hope their punishment is enough to stop any future incidents. I don't like them to suffer.'

'Earth, considering what they did to you, we had to do something. I'm hopeful.'

Earth bit her lip.

Justice stumbled off to bed, leaving Moon in charge. Moon promised to wake them if she was concerned for Earth's welfare again.

Now you've read my book
don't forget to review
Amazon, Goodreads,
Bookbub too!
Thank you very much
I'm counting on you!

Lily x

Acknowledgements

Thank you for reading my book.

I would like to thank Dreena Collins for the cover.

Thanks to Cheryl, Jo, and Dreena without whom you wouldn't be holding this book in your hands.

Thanks also to my betas and arcs.

To my Wordy's, my J's, TTAB and the Write Clubbers.

To Christine, Cin, and Anita.

To Butterfly whose colours grace my life.

And lastly to my Dad.

Thanks for everything.

About the Author

Lily Lawson is a poet and fiction writer
living in the UK.
She has poetry, short stories,
and creative non-fiction
published in anthologies and online
in addition to her books

You can find out more about Lily
and read more of her work on her blog.

Subscribers to Life with Lily
hear all her writing news.
You can sign up here.

Printed in Great Britain
by Amazon

45298119R00078